Shoot the Moon

MATT BEAM

orca soundings

ORCA BOOK PUBLISHERS

Published in Canada and the United States in 2025 by Orca Book Publishers.
orcabook.com

Library and Archives Canada Cataloguing in Publication
Title: Shoot the moon / Matt Beam.
Names: Beam, Matt, author.
Identifiers: Canadiana (print) 20240388070 | Canadiana (ebook) 20240388089 | ISBN 9781459839632 (softcover) | ISBN 9781459839649 (PDF) | ISBN 9781459839656 (EPUB)
Subjects: LCGFT: novels.
Classification: LCC PS8603.E352 S56 2025 | DDC jC813/.6—dc23

Library of Congress Control Number: 2024938994

Summary: Sixteen-year-old Charlie Abbott feels responsible for her father's mental health. When he takes off to go canoeing at a remote lake after a period of depression, she fears he's planning suicide, and goes after him.

Orca Book Publishers is committed to reducing the consumption of nonrenewable resources in the production of our books. We make every effort to use materials that support a sustainable future.

Orca Book Publishers gratefully acknowledges the support for its publishing programs provided by the following agencies: the Government of Canada, the Canada Council for the Arts and the Province of British Columbia through the BC Arts Council and the Book Publishing Tax Credit.

Design by Ella Collier.
Edited by Gabrielle Prendergast.
Cover artwork by Fran_Kies/Shutterstock.com.

Printed and bound in Canada.

28 27 26 25 • 1 2 3 4

To Sal

Chapter One

When I get home after school, all is okay. Closets are closed, pots and pans in place. There's no smell of burning. No sound from a radio so loud you can't think. Glass is still in the windows, the blinds on rods. The fridge is more or less full—with things that belong. This time.

I poke my head into the basement stairwell and listen. I hear the murmur of a radio. I can tell from the tone that it's talk radio. In some ways, it's a soothing sound to me because it means Dad is down there and he's listening to it. It means he's paying attention to the world around him. On his current set of bipolar meds, that doesn't happen all that often.

Which means I've had to pay attention to almost *everything*. Planning the meals. Shopping for food. Taking out the garbage. Making sure the bills get paid. I feel like I'm handling it all—but just barely.

Two months ago Dad fell into a dark depression—one side of bipolar disorder—and everything about him said *I don't want to be here.* Like, at all. Which is so hard.

But what I'm also worried about now is the other side of bipolar. The manic phase, a big emotional high. When Dad's like this, he's so up that he can't see the difference between realistic and downright dangerous. I noticed his dishes were put in the machine the other day and he's smiling more, which should be good, right? But now I'm worried about what he might get up to when I'm not around. Sometimes his state of mind changes really quickly. It's probably fine—we've just been through a lot over the last few years. I'm always a little on edge.

I pad down the stairs and knock softly.

"Come in, love," Dad says. He is sitting at his small desk, typing on his laptop. Again, this gives me joy. When he is down, Dad lies on his bed like a mummy, arms at his sides, eyes blank.

"Oh hey, Dad," I say. "Glad you're up."

He lowers the laptop's lid so I can't see what he's typing. "Up. Yes indeed," he says, swiveling around. "Who knew a two-letter word could pack so much punch."

I go to defend myself, to say I just meant up out of bed, but he breaks out in a big grin.

I love this smile. It's light and jokey. My shoulders start to lose their tension.

"It's great you are up and doing some work," I correct myself.

"Yeah, just catching up on a little something."

"Job-search stuff?" I ask.

"Sort of." A new smile appears on his face, and I'm not so sure about this one. It's mischievous, which can mean trouble, but I'll take it, especially because he's looking for work.

Two months ago, when he was depressed, Dad learned that he didn't get a job he was supposed to get teaching math at the university. I guess having the right degree and almost solving one of the biggest mathematical problems in the world aren't enough. He then stopped taking his pills and hid in the basement for a few weeks. He didn't change his clothes, didn't eat, didn't say a word to me.

I mean, I sort of understood. We really needed him to get that job. Mom can only put money in the joint account for so long. I don't know what changed, but he finally started taking his meds again.

"How was *your* day today, sweetheart?" he says now. I feel like he hasn't asked that question in weeks.

"Fine," I reply. "Hannah was absent today, so I just put my head down and worked."

Hannah is my best friend at my new high school. We met in the cafeteria line. She had just moved from Winnipeg, and we hit it off immediately. She knows about Dad—and Mom. She is my rock.

"I know I've not been exactly present these days, and I want to do something special for you. How about dinner tomorrow? I'm going to grab some garlic and anchovies at the store after a quick lunch with Jordan tomorrow."

Jordan is Dad's math pal, who he's been seeing more often, but shopping for food? I blink with happy surprise, but I try to contain it. "Let me guess," I say. "Your famous Caesar salad?"

He nods and grins. "Only the great Roman emperor made it better than me."

"Fun fact, Dad. No one ate side salads in a bowl two thousand years ago," I say. "But that would be great."

I study his face. His eyes are alive and, more important, present. I can't help but feel my spirits lifting.

Maybe we'll get out of this slump without tipping to the other side.

With this in mind, I give Dad a hug and go up to the kitchen to check that he has taken his meds. His daily medication box isn't beside the stove like usual, so it must be in his room, I think. Then my heart leaps when I see that the burner has been left on.

"Jeez, Dad," I say to myself. It's only on low, but still.

I turn the element off and convince myself it's easier saying nothing to Dad. Just then a text *ping* goes off on my phone.

Are you all right? I haven't heard from you today. My mom.

"Ugh," I moan and immediately delete the message. I can't text all day long. Mom has no idea how much I'm doing over here.

I step to the fridge and look inside for dinner fixings, but I can't get Mom off my mind.

It wasn't always like this. There was a time when we all lived together. Mom was happy at work. Dad was getting his PhD in Math. And I loved school and had lots of friends. But then, when it was taking too long for Dad to finally finish his degree, things went sideways. Mom was putting pressure on Dad to finish it, which seemed to send him into a deep depression and them into quarreling all the time.

And then, about a year and a half ago, my dad went to a hardware store with my mom's credit card. He bought hundreds of dollars' worth of building materials—to invent an energy machine using fusion.

It's not totally absurd to think he could. My dad is a genius. Not just with math but with engineering and stuff too. Anyway, when Mom and I got home there was a table saw in the living room and sparks flying everywhere.

"Not again. I can't do it. I can't do it!" Mom said that day.

She left him for good that night. I sort of understood. It was the first time I had seen mania right before my eyes. But I was also angry with her, and so sad for Dad. How could she just give up on him?

So I made a snap decision. I would live with my dad. The more Mom argued with me about this, the more I dug in my heels. I guess I'm stubborn like that. Dad and I found a new apartment together, which meant I also had to change schools.

That was sixteen months ago. And let's just say it hasn't been exactly smooth sailing since.

Chapter Two

"So I tried to talk to Lachlan in science class, but he was not a helpful lab partner," says Hannah the next day. "How some guys can talk about a rock song with such detail is beyond me."

Hannah is short and slim with black, straight hair. We are total opposites—I'm tall, blond and hazel-eyed. Not only that. Hannah's always trying to get me to loosen up a bit and take a chance. And she's a great listener. Kind of like the best parts of my parents wrapped up in one. Well, my mom *used* to listen, I guess.

"Anyway, I know you didn't ask me to talk to him, but he's in love with you. I just know it," Hannah says.

Enter another complication. Lachlan Tomic.

I guess it happened one day in math class. Lachlan was always near my desk, talking to his friend. One day he noticed me struggling over a functions question and asked if I needed help. I said no, several days in a row, but he was persistent, and in the end, he was so good at explaining it. I got the feeling he wasn't going to stop trying to teach me until I figured it out. Next thing you know, we were talking about other things every day.

Now I get butterflies every time I see him. Can you blame me? Lachlan's got wavy brown hair that hangs over his face and a cute button nose that crinkles when he smiles. He plays guitar in a band.

And when I look into his blue eyes, they always say the same thing—*I'm right here.*

So I should be excited about what Hannah said, but I'm distracted. She puts a hand on my shoulder and asks, "Hey, what's up? How's your dad?"

"He's okay," I say. "He's been out to talk math with a friend a couple of times. Like, actually left the house. So maybe he's turning things around."

I don't mention that this worries me too.

"Great," Hannah says with a laugh. "So now you can focus on you for a while...and Lachlan."

That evening Dad calls me to dinner. I see he has put out candles and wineglasses for our juice and soda. We only ever do this on special occasions. Sometimes when Dad cooks, the kitchen is a wild mess. Pots and pans everywhere. But tonight all the counters are clean.

"So not that I'm complaining," I say, glancing at the well-appointed table, "but what's the occasion?"

"I just thought I'd do something special."

I give him a cautious look. "Yes, but why special?"

"So...your exams are around the corner," he says, deflecting the question. He leans on his arm, and I see the six-inch scar on his forearm. From some teenage accident he's never fully explained. "How are you feeling about them?"

I see that Dad's changing the subject, but he's hit my soft spot. I always want to impress him, especially in math. "I need to do some serious studying if I want A's in functions."

"You know, a B never hurt anyone, even C's," he says. "Even Einstein got—"

"Oh, please with the Einstein, Dad. You know Mom will be all over me—us—if I'm not crushing it at school."

Dad smiles distantly and doesn't add another jab at Mom, which is strange.

"Tell me something else that's going on with you." The way he asks this makes me feel like I'm the only person in the world. It also feels like a challenge.

"Um, well...there's kind of a guy I like."

"Woo-hoo! That's a first at the new school, isn't it? Wow! It's been a while since I heard about a love interest. Amazing!"

"Yes, it is, but wait," I say, fighting off his charm. "You never answered my question. What's the special occasion?"

He looks at me for a long moment. He puts his hands on the table, like two spiders ready to leap.

"So...I have this theory. It all starts at the beginning. Yes, it's all the *beginning*. Like with math. If you make a mistake early on, you need to go back, because then if you go back to the start, way, way back, and fix that mistake, the problem is solved. It's all in the beginning."

He is speaking quickly.

"Are you working on a new math problem these days?" I ask. "Is that what you talked with Jordan about?"

"A problem, yes, but not—" He makes a face. A twitch of irritation. And it scares me a bit.

"Just a second," I say, getting up. "I need some water."

I go to the kitchen and check his pills again. The box is there now, and he's on schedule. With relief, I fill up my glass at the sink.

"Sorry," I say, returning. "You were saying?"

"No, it's nothing, Charlie. Just...a theory. Anyway, I really just want to hear more about this guy. Now don't get shy on me."

"His name is Lachlan. He's just a friend. He's barely a friend."

"Come on. How could he not adore my beautiful, brilliant daughter? Take a chance and tell your father the details," Dad says. "Shoot the moon with me, won't you?"

I smile. *Shoot the moon* is a term from the card game Hearts. Mom, Dad and I used to play it together all the time. It means going for broke to win it all even when there is little chance of doing so. Dad loved to shoot the moon when we played, even if it meant losing. I guess now he means I should spill about Lachlan and not worry about the consequences.

My phone buzzes in my pocket. I take a quick look. Five prying, annoying messages from my mom. I ignore them.

"Well," I finally answer him, "Lachlan is..." *Tall,* I think. *Freckled. Cute.* But Dad is not likely to care about those things. "...good at math," I try. "He helps me sometimes with my functions homework."

A shadow falls over my dad's face. I've made a mistake. Math is like his best friend and his enemy. His frenemy. And because of that, he has trouble talking to me about it.

"He's also really, really nice," I say quickly. "And funny."

He nods distantly. "That's great, honey. You deserve the very, very best."

This doesn't land. I look at my dad, who is starting to eat his food but is clearly elsewhere.

Where has he gone?

Chapter Three

My heart leaps when I find Lachlan standing outside my science classroom the next day. I need the distraction.

"Hey, Charlie," Lachlan says. "What's up?"

"Hi," I just barely manage to say.

"So," he says, "I was wondering if you'd like to, you know, go out for a smoothie this weekend."

My heart stops.

I would love to, but I immediately think about being away from Dad. It's a reflex.

"It's possible, but...I just need to check—"

"Lach!"

Lachlan looks a bit hurt as he turns to his best friend, Vijay.

"Tossing the ball on the field in two," Vijay declares.

"I'm there," Lachlan replies, deepening his voice just a little, which I find kind of cute.

My phone pings.

"You need to get that. And I gotta go," he says gently. "Mmm, smoothies. Think about it."

He gives my wrist an affectionate squeeze.

I can't even help myself. I'm moving toward him, but Lachlan doesn't notice and walks away.

I hold my head and then I pull out my phone. It's a message from my mom.

I'm coming to take you to lunch at noon. We need to talk.

Hannah is in the library, deep into a textbook, when I find her.

"Hey, what're you studying for?" I say. I'm lightheaded, my mind on Lachlan.

"Bio," Hannah replies, and then sizes me up with a grin. "He asked you on a date, didn't he? Just like I told him to. Your face is bright red!"

"I didn't think you were actually going to suggest it," I say, collapsing in a seat. "And I could have used a warning."

"I didn't have time," she explains. "Anyway, you *do* want to go out with him, don't you?"

"Of course! But my dad...I don't know. There's something up with him. He said something about starting at the beginning of a problem. But I don't know what kind of problem he's talking about."

"Maybe he wants to start over with you."

"Anyway, he seems good for once, and that feels, well, good. Oh yeah—She-Devil is coming for lunch."

"Interesting," Hannah says. "What does your mother want?"

"I don't know. She rarely needs a reason to just barge into my life, right?"

"Let's talk about happier things." She makes a stupid face. "Like Lachlan."

Lachlan. I replay the conversation with him. "I think I almost kissed him today. Like, right there in the hallway."

"What?!" Hannah yelps.

A bunch of shhhhhs come from the library stalls.

"That's insane!" she whispers.

"He didn't see me moving toward him," I say, shaking my head. "Or maybe he did and wasn't interested."

"Charlie, he turned redder than a tomato when I said...well, you know, what I said."

"What *did* you say?"

She just smiles. "Apparently the right thing."

"Usually I don't like people meddling in my business," I say. "But you're just so darned good at it, Hannah." I look at my watch. "Sorry, I've got to run."

"Good luck with She-Devil."

"Good luck with studying."

Mom's staring at her cell phone when I get in the car.

"Hi, honey," she says nicely, but I sense tension. "How are you?"

"Fine," I reply coldly. "How are you?"

"Okay, I guess," she says with a big sigh. "Ever since I took the promotion, I barely have a moment to myself. This is nice though."

"Why are you here, Mom?"

"I just wanted to see you and...I'm worried. Your marks are slipping, and your father just doesn't—I feel like things have been spiraling ever since your dad didn't get the job. Am I wrong?"

I did miss a few important days of school, but I'm not going to admit that.

"You are wrong."

She looks out the window. "How is your dad anyway? He sent me a message yesterday for the first time in ages."

I want to tell her about last night, because she'd be the only one who would really understand, but nothing actually happened. Except that I've got this tense feeling in my stomach.

"He's fine."

She turns on the car and starts to drive. "Where do you want to eat?"

"I don't care. I brought my lunch."

"What about work for your dad?"

"What about it?"

"He needs a job. For him, for you, for all of us. It took him ten years to get his PhD. How long do you think it'll take for him to apply for a job? Sorry, it's just—"

"He's already applied to the one at the university. It's not his fault he didn't get it."

"Are you sure?" she challenges, hands gripping the wheel tight.

"Am I sure what?"

"Well, I happened to be chatting with one of Dad's old colleagues, and he said he hadn't seen his application—"

"You were spying on Dad?"

She takes a deep breath. "I'm sorry, Charlie. We just...need to talk more. There are things you don't know. About your dad...and about me. I'm not going to be available this wee—"

"Why do you always assume I don't know about Dad? I know him better than you. I'm the one who's been living with him for almost a year and a half, and I'm not the one who bailed on him."

Mom drives silently for a while. "I know you don't want to hear this," she says finally, "but there are things happening in my life too—"

"Sorry, I just can't do this right now, Mom. Just stop the car."

She doesn't put on the brakes.

"I said 'Stop the car!'"

"Don't yell at me, Charlie. I will when it's safe."

My heart is pounding. She finally pulls over. I open the door and jump out. As I slam the door, I hear her call my name.

I turn toward school, but I don't want to go back. There is a park on the way home, and that's the direction I go. In my head, as I walk the streets, I hear my mother call my name again, my father's name, my grandpa's name. All of us named Charlie.

Chapter Four

When I get home, I realize I'm pretty worked up, but the last thing I want is another fight, especially with Dad. Even so, I go to the top of the basement stairs to make sure he is there. I hear the radio playing.

Good. He's listening.

I make a sandwich and sit down at the kitchen table. As I eat, I think about what Mom said about us talking more. What did she mean? What does she have to tell me?

But I also realize that I want this. I'm lonely. I want more communication between us, and maybe I'm ready for it.

I don't know. Maybe not. If she could just back off a little.

I look at my phone:

How was she-devil? An earlier text from Hannah.

I don't respond, because I wonder if the nickname is really fair.

When I'm done eating, I decide I'll check on Dad after all. But when I push open his door, he's not there. The bed is not made, and there is a note perched on his comforter. It says *Charlie, I've gone on a little trip. Love always and forever, Dad.*

A trip? Where? I feel panicked. The only trip he's been on in the last year has been to the café to meet Jordan.

I open Dad's laptop and put in his password. I know it because he told me. Sort of a safety-slash-trust thing. I've never needed to use it before. At least, not without him knowing.

His password is *chuckie*, a nickname from his childhood. Chuckie stories are always funny and full of grade-school pranks, and they always make him smile. I go through his contacts. I punch *Jordan* into the search box. The first email that pops up just says *See you soon*. Below that it says *Jordan Perez, she/her.*

Jordan is a woman?!

My heart pounds as I dial the phone number in the email. It goes straight to voice mail, which gives her office hours at the university—2 to 4 p.m. on Tuesdays and Fridays. Her voice is deep and soothing.

I look at my phone. If I hurry I can catch her.

As I move the cursor to close the window, my eye catches an email from my mom. It says *Charlie missed school again today. Did you know that? And what's this new theory of yours? It concerns me. Remember I'm busy this weekend. With my life getting more complicated, I need to know you are taking care of her.*

More complicated? What is she talking about? And is this theory the same one Dad shared with me at dinner? Anxiety shoots through me.

I search the room for clues. I strip his bed and find nothing. There's nothing on the walls or in the laundry hamper.

Then a thought strikes me. I go to the kitchen. Dad's med box is sitting there. I check. He didn't take his pills yesterday!

My hands are shaking.

I realize suddenly that I don't really know what pills he's taken. If he wanted to, he could have added to or subtracted from the main bottles in the bathroom cabinet. He could have been off them for weeks.

I run to the bathroom and shake his bottle. It's full, but this is futile—I can't even remember when the prescription was last filled.

I'm trying not to panic, but I have a very bad feeling. I call Jordan one more time, but it clicks into voice mail again.

I decide I'll go to the university to find her. In the kitchen, I force down a banana and grab a muffin. I go upstairs to my room and get my money pouch, which has ten bucks, my ID and my subway card. I keep my mom's Visa in a separate place, so I don't go on a spending spree.

I think about whether to grab it. I shake my head and try to calm myself. This is all just a misunderstanding. I will find Dad very soon, and he will start to take his pills tonight at dinner.

I leave the house in a hurry and run to the subway.

The mathematics department is like a ghost town. I walk the squeaky hallways, looking for her office. Just then a door opens down the hallway, and a woman approaches. She is strikingly beautiful, and she looks in a hurry.

"Jordan Perez," I say.

"That's Dr. Perez to you," she replies with a smile, like we are friends already. But I don't think I want to be her friend.

"I'm looking for Charlie Abbott. I'm—"

"Charlie Abbott," she interjects, and we both laugh awkwardly. "You look just like him. Yes, I actually just saw him recently."

"Where? When? Like, today?" I ask. "I really need to find him."

"Not today. Yesterday."

"Yeah, I knew about that, but I didn't know you were *you*."

She makes a coy smile I don't like at all.

"Okay, new question. Who the hell are you to my dad?"

"We met about a year and a half ago," she explains. "Here in the department."

My stomach tightens. I can already see it. Dad being enchanting, because he can't even help it, and

Jordan falling hard. How could he do this to me? And to Mom?

"So you told math jokes in the department lounge?" I say.

"No," she says, "I just found myself around him because...because he had a certain gravitational pull. Your dad is funny and goofy, and deep down he's just a good guy."

I agree, but I can barely hear her—my mind is spinning. "Okay, so when was this exactly? When did this start?"

"February, two Februarys ago," she replies.

My parents broke up two months later. Because of this woman? So it wasn't the flying-sparks fusion-machine disaster that caused their breakup?

I can see Mom's face from then, tense and unhappy, and I suddenly understand it better. "So Mom knows about you?" I ask.

"Yes. Your mom found out somehow and confronted your father. She was very mature about it all."

Despite how I feel about Mom these days, I can see it. She is pretty practical.

"So you caused their separation," I say. It's not a question.

"No, Charlie, I don't think I did."

I want to argue with her, but I know she is right.

"I saw your father a few more times after that, and then he just disappeared. I didn't hear from him until recently."

"This isn't happening." I put my face in my hands. "Where is my dad? What did he say yesterday?" I ask.

"Not much. He said goodbye. He hugged me and then he was gone."

"What *exactly* did he say to you?" I ask. "The exact words?"

"Well, I guess he did say something a little strange. He said he was 'shooting the moon.'"

Chapter Five

Shooting the moon. The phrase hits me in the gut. First because Dad shared a special family ritual with this...stranger. I realize we haven't played a game of Hearts since Mom and Dad split up. Since Jordan came into his life.

But then I take a breath and try to understand what he was saying to her. In the card game, it means to get all thirteen hearts and the queen of spades to win it all. But what does that mean in his life?

"What do you think he meant?" I ask her.

"Well, I just thought he meant daring to take on mathematics again. He's had quite a break from it."

"He was talking about a problem," I say, "but it's not math. What did he seem like when he came here?"

"Excited," she says, then frowns. "No, *over*excited. He said he had figured something out but wouldn't explain. Again, I thought it was about math."

"Last night he said something about going back to the beginning. That if you correct an earlier mistake, it can fix everything."

"Over the last few months, your dad was different. Sad. He talked about you a lot. He was so sorry when he missed your music performance in the spring."

"The spring concert? I was pretty irritated but—"

"I guess he just really wanted to be there for you—and couldn't always. And he *wanted* to apply for the university job, but after taking so long on his degree, he wasn't feeling confident."

"No! He told me he—"

She shakes her head sadly, which makes me furious. Both Mom and Jordan know more about him than I do.

"So...you two basically had an affair?"

She grimaces. "Yes, but I think I was just giving your dad a break from...his life."

"You mean he needed a break from me?!"

"No, Charlie," she insists. "He loves you so, so much. The truth is, he sometimes wondered if you needed a break from him."

How dare he! I'm the one who decides if I need a break! I can't believe it.

"So where has he gone to then, if he loves me so much?"

"I'm worried too, Charlie," she says. "Maybe he's home right now. Why don't you call him?"

"I would, but he never answers."

"Why don't you go home and check?"

My brain whirls.

"I don't know how much I'm helping," Jordan says. "Wait. There's something else he said that stood out. He said he might visit 'the palace.'"

The palace? Grandpa's place? That's what Grandpa pridefully called his cottage home in the country.

"Okay," I say. I find my grandpa in my contacts and press *call.*

"Hello, Charlie. Is that you?"

"Yes. Hi, Grandpa. This might sound strange, but is Dad at the palace?"

"No, honey, but funny thing. He left a message on my machine saying he was thinking about going to our old stomping ground."

"What stomping ground?"

"Well, there's a couple of places I can think of. Maybe across the lake and through the rapids, or maybe Calm Lake. Would help if the man carried a cell phone, wouldn't it."

I wish Grandpa was more mobile these days, so he could check, but he can't paddle alone anymore.

I think for a moment. My gut is telling me there's only one thing to do. Shoot the moon.

"I'm going to come up tonight, Grandpa. I need to make sure he's all right."

"Your father can camp on his own just fine, honey. And he only said he was thinking about it. What about your mother?"

"I'll talk to her. And I'll call you back. Thanks, Grandpa."

"Okay."

I turn to Jordan, who has been just standing there. "Can you check to see if there are any buses to Huntsville tonight? I don't have data."

Jordan nods and checks her phone. After a minute, she announces, "There's a bus leaving at six."

"It's four fifty-five right now," I say, looking at my phone. Another thought strikes.

"One sec," I say, and text Hannah.

you there?

After a few seconds I get a text back.

aren't I always?

can you go to my house? I need help.

can't right now. need to get home to help my parents with shopping. why?

I think of Lachlan. Maybe he can help. But then I think about him being exposed to all of this, to my life, to my sick dad. But my relationship with Lachlan is probably doomed anyway.

Now I'm really shooting the moon.

Chapter Six

I find Lachlan's number and type while Jordan waits patiently beside me.

hey lachlan, it's charlie. really strange question, but are you home right now?

hi! yep, i'm here. what's up?

i need a weird favor. can you knock on my door at home? i need to check if my dad is there.

surrrrre. you live on Trenton Ave, right?

He knew this?

yes, 27. knock really loudly and wait. if he's there, then just ask if I'm there and go home. easy. if he isn't...wait for further instructions, Agent Tomic ;)

I wait nervously.

yessir!

Nice!

I look up at Jordan, who is watching me intently.

"You're reminding me of your father," she says. "What are you cooking up, Charlie?"

"It's too complicated to explain, and I am *not* my father."

Saying this feels good. The border between he and I has been so blurry these days—and I feel like I want me back.

"Okay," Jordan says. "I'm sorry, but I don't think I'm helping anymore, and I'm late for that appointment. Here's my number if there's anything I can do. And Charlie, for what it's worth, I'm sorry."

"Thanks, Jordan," I say and force a smile.

A text comes through as she walks away. It's Lachlan.

no answer

I take a deep breath and press *call.*

"Hi there."

Lachlan's voice is so sweet!

"Hi, Lachlan. Sorry about this! But before we begin this mission, I've got another strange question, if you're up for it."

"This sounds fun."

"Are you free for the next hour? And you drive, right?"

"Um, I was supposed to be studying for exams, but I do have a car so...sure, I'm free."

I smile. Not only is he cute, he's generous—and adventurous.

"Thank you so much. Do you think you could bring a few things to the bus station for me?"

"Okay, really, are you a secret agent?"

"Ha ha. Something like that."

"Well, in that case, for sure then!"

I laugh. "The key is under the flower pot on the porch."

"Who would have guessed?"

"I know. The most unlikely hiding place in the world, right? And created by my genius mathematician dad."

"Your dad's a mathematician? Cool."

"Yeah," I say. But strangely I feel a bit sad. I wish it were as cool as it sounds.

"Hey, you okay over there?"

"Um, yeah. It's complicated."

"All right, I've got the key. I'm in."

"Can you call out a hello? Sometimes my dad ignores knocks on the door."

He does as I say, and we both wait a few moments. "Nothing. Where is your dad, Charlie?"

"That's the problem. I'm not sure."

"And you need help finding him? I'm in."

I melt a little. "Okay," I say, staying focused. "There's a box of pills on the kitchen counter. Can you grab them?"

"Sure." And then, ten seconds later, "Got 'em."

"Great. Now there's a credit card in a red box in my room."

There is a long pause as I hear him moving around, which makes me realize the complete insanity of it all. Lachlan Tomic in my room, alone, seeing my personal life. Was my room even clean?

"Just so you know, Charlie, I'm not snooping."

He reads minds too—and lies well.

"It's okay." I lie well too.

"All right, I've got the pills and the card."

"Great."

What else? I get another idea.

"I need you to go down to the basement. There's a desk and laptop."

"No problem."

I hear him going down the stairs.

"Okay, now this might sound even stranger, but I need you to look through my father's laptop."

"Um, are you sure?"

This is sweet. But I realize I really trust Lachlan.

"Yes, if you are okay with it. This is a bit of an emergency."

"I get it. Okay, it's open."

"The password is *chuckie*. Go to his browser history. And just look to see if there's anything suspicious there."

"Right, okay, I'm here. Opening up browser. There's a car-rental page and there's another link to a canoe outfitting company, White Pine."

"Hmm, okay. What's the address?"

"County Road 23, Algonquin Park."

"That's it. Okay, we need to hurry. I'm sorry this is all so rushed, but can you get to the bus station in, like, thirty minutes?"

"I got my driver's license two months ago, so I won't speed or anything, but I think I can make it!"

"Thank you sooooo much, Lachlan. See you soon."

Chapter Seven

I'm at the bus station. It's five forty, and there is no sign of Lachlan.

I feel a sudden burst of anxiety that he won't make it.

It's five forty-three.

My phone buzzes.

I look at it. My mom. **You okay?**

I shrug. **Yes**, I text back.

The phone rings.

It's her. I don't know what to say. If I don't pick

up, she will hound me all night. But I don't know how or where to start. The phone rings again. My thumb hovers. I want to protect Dad, but I know that's insane.

I press down and I say hello, but the call must have clicked into voice mail.

The station doors suddenly swing open and a young man enters, but it's not Lachlan. It's five fifty.

I text Hannah. **Lachlan checked house. Dad not there. I'm going to my grandpa's. I think he's headed that way.**

Why wouldn't he have just told you that?

I don't know. remember that math friend he had, Jordan? SHE's my dad's lover.

What?!?!?

Yeah. sorta caused my parents' separation.

Uhhh. that's totally not cool.

No sign of Lachlan. I get in the ticket line anyway.

Gotta go. I'll text from bus.

I stare at the front doors of the station, willing Lachlan to appear. I am next in line. It's five fifty-five.

The woman with the big glasses behind the glass calls out, "Next."

I step forward and then glance back. No Lachlan. "Um...I need one ticket to Huntsville, please."

She clicks the keyboard with a series of strokes. Still no one.

"Okay," she says. "The six o'clock for one student?"

"Y-e-s," I reply, drawing the word out.

"Forty-two fifty, please."

I turn back and there he is, searching for me.

"Lachlan!" I call out.

He pivots, locates me and smiles. I feel a rush of happiness.

"Hey, Charlie," he says, hurrying up to me. "Sorry I'm late. Traffic was insane."

"It's totally okay. But I need my stuff right now."

"Miss, are you going to pay or not? There are people waiting."

"Here," Lachlan says, handing me a plastic bag. "It's all in there."

"Thank you!" I say. I search out the card and hand it to the lady.

I turn to Lachlan. "I'm sorry we didn't have that smoothie before you got dragged into my stupid family life. Maybe we can do something next week?"

"It's totally fine," he says. "But is everything, like, okay, Charlie?"

I blink away sudden tears. He wants to help. I want help. But I can't get him stuck in this mess.

"Miss? The bus won't wait for you," the ticket seller says.

"I'm fine," I lie to Lachlan, grabbing my ticket. "It's just a little thing between me and my dad."

"Is he in danger?"

I shrug. This gives me a lump in my throat.

"Okay," he says, "text me when you're on the bus."

"Got it," I agree, and I want to hug him but somehow can't. I glance at my phone. Six o'clock.

I give Lachlan my best smile, and I then turn and run toward the bus.

The bus is packed. I sit beside an old woman with a big blue purse on her lap. I text Lachlan. **On! thanks again!**

I lean back and notice my heart is racing. Is that how love works? In years past I liked a few guys, and kind of had a few "boyfriends," but this feeling is completely different. When he looks at me, I feel it. He really sees me, like no one else has seen me before.

I stare at my phone and will him to respond to me, but he is probably driving, so it's smart that he doesn't. I feel like I've just taken a drug, and I can't trust my thoughts.

I text Hannah. **Lachlan made it. on bus now. I wanted to hug him to death.**

But you didn't.

Yeah, we have yet to break the hug barrier ;)

I lean back and sigh.

"Where are you off to?"

It's the lady beside me. "Um, sorry, what?" I reply.

"You almost missed the bus. Are you going home?"

"Yeah," I lie. Back off lady, I think.

"Barrie?"

"No, Huntsville," I say.

She slowly looks me up and down. "You look like you are on the run."

"Well, I'm not," I snap at her.

A message comes in. It's my mom. My heart leaps as I scan the words. **I love you.**

This *love you* sneaks through the cracks in my armor. I blink back tears. She does love me. And I need help—plus I have so many questions for her about Jordan and Dad. And then there's Lachlan and the feelings I'm having—Mom would have advice. Good advice. I miss her.

I text her back. **Love you too.**

I stare at the phone for a response, but it says she has turned off her notifications. I could call her right now, but I'm struggling with how to explain and not create a disaster.

I really just want to talk—to someone.

"It's not me," I say to the old woman. "It's my father who ran away."

She turns to me with interest. "Why?" she asks kindly.

"Well, because he's sick," I admit. "And now I have to find him."

"Oh," she says, sounding confused.

All of a sudden I feel vulnerable.

"Excuse me, I need to go to the washroom," I say, getting up.

The washroom smells like it has never been cleaned. I grab the handle on the wall and make a call on my phone. After a few rings, a voice says, "Hello?"

"Hi, Grandpa," I say. "I'm coming. Six o'clock bus."

"Does your mom know?"

"I'm going to call her right now. See you soon."

I lean against the door and think of Charles, my grandpa. Every summer until they split up, and for as long as I can remember, Mom and Dad would leave me at his cottage for a week to get a break from parenting. Some kids went to camp. I went to Grandpa's. He would take me on overnight canoeing trips. And he was tough, always barking orders like I was in the military. At these times, it sometimes felt like he was mistaking me for my dad. When Mom and Dad came to pick me up, I remember Dad would always get out last and stand at a distance. He had trouble with Grandpa.

A text comes in. It's Lachlan. **Are you sure you are okay? Is there anything I can do?**

My heart swells. He can't help. No one can.

I now feel a desperate need to reach out to my mom. I press *call* on her number. The phone rings five times and then clicks into voice mail. I panic and hang up.

She'll call back right away. Mom always has her phone. For work, for me, for anything at all. I wait, standing in the stinking bathroom, trying not to lean on the counter.

I wait a minute. No reply.

Two minutes. Still none.

At three I decide I can't stand the stink any longer. I open the bathroom door and shuffle down the aisle.

As I sit back in my seat, I remember in her email to Dad she said she was busy, but she's always busy. *Why isn't she answering?*

Chapter Eight

Grandpa is waiting at Huntsville bus station, his face hidden under the shadow of his cap. "Is that all you have?" he says, looking at my money pouch and the plastic bag Lachlan brought me.

"I was a little rushed," I say without stepping in for a hug. I'm used to his coolness.

We don't say anything else as we make our way to the truck, the same truck he's had for years. As I sit in the worn passenger seat, I realize that the last time I did this, I didn't even know Mom and Dad were splitting up.

"So what are you studying in math these days?" he asks awkwardly, as the truck ignition struggles to catch. Unlike Dad, he actually loves to talk about math—and pretty much nothing else.

"Functions," I reply with a sigh. "They're hard."

"Functions?" he says with sudden glee as the truck finally roars to life. "Functions are my favorite. What could be more functional than a function. It's applied in this tank of gas, in the speed—"

"Grandpa," I interrupt. "I'm worried about Dad. We need to find him."

He nods. "I agree, but it's too late to do anything safely. Your father is a skilled outdoorsman." He pauses, not saying the rest. That Dad will be fine. That I shouldn't worry too much. "I left a message with your mom. Told her your father went on a trip on his own and you've come to get him."

"You what?" Deep down I'm happy he did this. I wonder now if we should call the police too. I'm pretty sure this is what you do in these situations, but Grandpa is so certain about Dad's safety and the way forward.

"Yes, I called your mother. I didn't want to ask you to call her a third time. Truth is, I'm more worried about you than I am your father. You can't protect him forever, honey."

I don't respond. I don't want to hear this, but I'm relieved. I'm okay, so Dad must be too. I know this isn't logical, but it soothes me. I close my eyes for a moment.

"Anyway, so where were we? Functions, yes, they are everywhere. They're in..."

As my grandpa talks, my mind drifts to my father and his relationship with math. It is a knot inside his head. It is a knot he has fussed over and fought with and loved for all of his life. At some point, maybe when I was seven or eight, after I'd mastered the basic stuff, he just stopped talking to me about math. It was Mom who had to help me with my homework. In the end, she wasn't exactly fun to sit with over a fractions problem.

But she did it. And I don't think I ever gave her credit for that.

Finally we arrive at the driveway, marked by the tin mailbox. The leaves brush the sides of the creaking truck as it bumps in toward the cottage. There's a weird smell coming from the engine, but I don't want to say anything about Grandpa's precious baby.

Inside, Grandpa yawns and says, "It's late, Charlie. We'll head out first thing tomorrow. You can stay in your room—your father's old one. Okay?"

"Okay. Good night." I desperately want a hug now, but I know that's not the way Grandpa rolls.

As soon as I close the door to my room, I plug in my phone. It is beyond dead.

I lie back and stare at the ceiling. I sit up and look at the phone.

It's at 1 percent and there are no bars. I forgot this place was in a bad pocket.

I click off the light and fall back again. I think about my dad and his dad. Charlie and Charles, pretty much not talking to each other, and how sad it is. Did Grandpa give up on Dad, or was it the other way around? I've always tried to impress Dad, and he did the same with his father once.

In a dreamy, impossible way, it feels like everything is coming clear suddenly, that everything is solvable. I imagine Dad saying the word *solvable.* Is it Dad's word...or is it Mom's?

It doesn't seem to matter, as I gently drift away into sleep.

Chapter Nine

"Earth to Charlie! Up now. Let's go," Grandpa announces, standing over me. "I think I might know where your dad is."

I drag myself out of bed, grab my phone and follow him dutifully out the door. It's dawn. We step outside. The lake greets me silently, a patch of fog still hanging over it.

I creak onto the dock behind him. Grandpa turns and gets himself carefully into the stern. The bow, the front, is for me. To keep pace. Even and easy. And to watch for rocks.

Without a word we start paddling. My shoulder is tight, and my stroke feels wrong.

I take a quick break to check my phone. Still no bars.

Taking in a deep breath, I try to relax. There are other cottages on the lake, but their windows are sleepy. I feel like we're all alone. The distant sound of the rapids draws us in. It feels like it is calling to us.

"When your father was about your age, he had this idea," Grandpa says behind me. "The water levels here were really high at the lake, and he had some notion for a sort of drainage system."

"Sounds like him."

"He was trying to impress me."

I nod.

"But it was two in the morning when he had his big idea," he says, sounding annoyed. "So he walked six miles into town and tried to break the glass library door to get some book on fusion he'd seen. As in, right through it. Shoulder first."

"Jeez!" I say, turning.

"That's right. You know that scar on his arm?"

"The one on his right forearm? I guess I always thought it was from a childhood prank."

"The RCMP were not exactly understanding. But he was stitched up at the hospital and eventually things were sorted out. I took him on a canoe trip right away, which might not have been the right call. I don't know. But something happened out there. He wasn't well, and he just closed off. Your grandma was much better at dealing with your dad's ups and downs."

"You mean his bipolar disorder."

"Right, like what happened a year and a half ago."

He paddles silently for a moment.

"I just...I just don't understand," he says. "You and your mom...you have always been so close."

"I guess."

"No guessing about it," he insists. "Whenever I think of you, you are with your mom, in each other's arms on the couch, snuggling and giggling."

I let this sink in. When did it stop? Not at the divorce—earlier. What was it? I was younger, maybe twelve or thirteen. There's nothing, no event, I can connect to this.

"Right," I allow finally. "And...and where's Dad at these times?"

"On the lake? In the woods? I don't know, but he's not with you two."

"He's avoiding you too probably," I say.

"Maybe," Grandpa allows.

As I think about this, I hear a dull roar. I can see the river and some rapids ahead. My heart rate goes up. There is something about the power of water that is terrifying. I can now see a thin, foamy line on the surface of the water as the shores narrow.

At first Grandpa is heading toward the beach, but then he veers. I look back.

"Grandpa?" I say. "Where are we going?"

"Don't worry," he answers. "It's easier than carrying the canoe over. The water is high, so it shouldn't be a problem. Keep your eyes open for smooth rushing water—that's where the big rocks are."

I bend low in the boat. The current picks up. We are now moving faster than we can paddle. Grandpa is right—the water is high, so there aren't many rocks to be seen. Still, with high water comes speed. You don't need an equation to figure this out—it is real and in front of us. Grandpa is sterning us, so he's in control. But as bowsperson, I'm in charge of sudden moves. The desperate ones.

I see a smooth rush of water on my right and point with my paddle. I glance back. He's wearing a grin that reminds me of my father. We are heading straight for a whale of a rock. I do a move with my paddle. I can't remember the name of the move, but when I do it, we jerk out of the way at the last second. I watch as we just miss the gray rock below.

Chapter Ten

Finally the rapids run themselves out, and we paddle to the shore. We get out of the canoe, and he points across this new small lake to a campsite. There's a yellow tent and two kids fishing on the shore. "He's not here."

"What about farther in?" I ask.

"No, it just gets swampier from here."

"This isn't the place you took Dad, is it?"

"Well, I did a few times, but you're right. It's not the place I mentioned earlier."

"Then why did you bring me here? Don't you realize how serious this is?"

"For two reasons. First off, I wasn't going to send you out into the wilderness on your own without making sure you still had it."

"Had what?"

"Well, the paddling—and the solo portaging skills. My back can't do canoe-carrying anymore."

I look back at the path, a portage that snakes back along the river and connects the two lakes when the water is too low for a canoe to pass through.

"What's the second reason?"

"Because your mother should be on her way right now. I told her she should come. You just can't do this all on your own anymore, Charlie. Your father cannot take care of you, and you are better off living with your mom."

"No I'm not," I snap. "You don't know anything about our lives."

"He said so himself just a month ago."

"He said what himself?"

"Your father said he can't do it anymore."

"Do what?"

"Take care of you. It's too much for him, and now that your mom has a new boyfriend, she won't be able to check in as much."

I turn away, my face flushing with the shock of this news.

"You didn't know," he says gently.

"No, I didn't," I say. "And Dad didn't say that—there's no way. Besides, I'm the one who is doing everything!" I press my thumb into my chest, fighting tears.

"Exactly. You've had to take so much," Grandpa agrees gently. "And you shouldn't have had to. Because look"—he throws his arms in the air—"there's another emergency, and here's where you end up."

"What do you mean, *another emergency*?" I snap.

He stares through me for a moment and then shrugs his shoulders. "Remember the time when you were about twelve and we decided to keep you for an extra week so we could go on a longer trip?"

"Yes," I say. *When I was twelve...when Mom and I became distant...or stressed.*

"Your father swallowed a bottle of pills."

"What?!"

"Your dad was admitted to the hospital for the week, and your mom told us to keep you. They said they were going to tell you, but I guessed they wouldn't. Your mother has been protecting your dad ever since they were together—well, until she finally left him."

My body is tense and my mind numb, but I have an energy that feels like it is going to explode.

I need to find Dad. I bend over and struggle to lift the canoe.

"That's it," Grandpa says. "Now remember. It's all about rocking the canoe. Right hand low, left high. Lift and roll."

I don't want to listen, but I need this to work. Without another thought, I lift the canoe to my thighs and roll the canoe up. I struggle to level it with my right arm.

I stagger a bit, but somehow I steady myself.

The canoe is on my shoulders.

I feel proud, despite my new anger and overwhelming fear about Dad.

When we make it back to the other lake, I practically fling the canoe back into the water. Grandpa nods his head in approval.

"Well, if your mother doesn't make it here in time to stop you, at least I know you can do it."

While we silently paddle back, my brain is churning.

My mom has a new boyfriend. My father tried to kill himself four years ago. My parents—both of them—are liars.

That explains why Mom didn't answer my text. She's moved on, and now Dad is moving on too. I can't even think about what this might mean.

I throw anger and fear into every stroke until we arrive at the dock.

"Dad didn't take his meds with him," I blurt out, "and I can't believe you wasted all this time and... and..."

I flee the dock for the cottage, leaving the pulling-out of the canoe for Grandpa, and I hear him call me. I lurch into the cottage through the screened-in porch.

When I get to my room, I throw myself on my bed. And that's when I hear it.

A voice calling out.

I think I'm imagining it.

It can't be.

Chapter Eleven

I wipe my face and run out to the back door. When I open it, I almost fall over.

It's Lachlan standing by his car, a big grin on his face. "I'm here!" he announces.

"Wha—what are you doing here?"

"You didn't see my texts?" He sees my swollen eyes.

"Um, no."

"I just...I just knew you were in trouble, Charlie," he says apologetically, "and I just kinda knew you wouldn't ask for help. Like, how long did it take you to finally accept my help in math?"

I'm in shock but also amazed that he's here. "But...how did you find me?" Then I look over my shoulder. Grandpa still isn't back. And Mom hasn't arrived.

I realize I'm not ready for her to.

"Hannah knew your grandpa's name," he explains, "and there's only one C. Abbott in Huntsville."

I'm only half listening.

"We need to go," I say. "Like, right now."

"But what about your grandpa?"

"Another time," I say and hurry to the passenger door.

"Okay," he says reluctantly and goes to the driver's side.

We both get in, and Lachlan starts the car. As he swings up the driveway, I glance back. There's still no sign of Grandpa. I hope he's okay.

I hear pinging from my phone.

"Just a sec," I say as Lachlan drives. I pull out my phone. There's a stream of texts from Hannah and Lachlan.

Okay, fasten your seat belt bc I think Lachlan is on his way to you.

Hi Charlie. It might seem a little strange but I talked to Hannah and I think you need help. I'm coming to find you. You are at your grandpa's? In Barrie. Still coming. It's county road 6, right?

Then three from Mom, first an answer to last night's text. **You called?**

Then **What's going on?**

And then **Stay there. I'm coming to get you.**

I realize I am furious at my mother now for a whole new set of reasons, but I still feel for her in a way that I haven't for years. My mind is a mess.

I take a deep breath. "I just got your texts," I say to Lachlan, "and a few from my mom."

"Okay," Lachlan says patiently. I can tell he has

questions but is holding back.

The car emerges from the woods, and we are now heading toward town.

"So," Lachlan says, "I should drive to White Pine outfitters now or...?"

"Yes. I mean no. I mean, so much is happening right now," I say, feeling overwhelmed. "I need to process it all. But before we do anything more, I really need food. Like, really, really. How about a drive-through?"

"We can definitely do that," Lachlan agrees, putting a hand on my leg, and I realize what I really need is a hug but instead I put my hand on his until he has to make a turn.

I devour the takeout breakfast sandwich, and Lachlan continues toward the park and the outfitters.

"So," I say, "I just found out that my mother has a boyfriend."

"Wow," Lachlan says. "That's...was it a surprise?"

"Yeah." I want to say more, but my throat is tight.

There is an awkward silence in the car.

"So I don't know if this will help with anything, Charlie," Lachlan begins, "but I was thinking about my brother on the way up here."

"You have a brother?" I'm relieved at the change of subject.

"Yeah, Sam. He's twelve and the best. But he has ADHD pretty bad, so he really struggles at school and with some social stuff. Sam was teased, and he couldn't control himself so he was constantly getting in scraps."

I picture this little version of Lachlan and it makes me want to escape to the park with the two of them—forever.

"I stuck up for him, and then one day he came to my room and told me I had to stop protecting him. He said he had to fight his own battles."

"He's twelve and he said that?" I say in disbelief.

"He was eight at the time," Lachlan replies. "Told you he was smart. Anyway, my parents found a better school for him, and he's been doing much better. But Sam still keeps my parents pretty busy, so—"

"—that's why they let you do whatever you want," I interrupt. "Like drive to Huntsville for no reason on a study weekend."

"Exactly." Lachlan nods with a grin. "The point being that by telling me to stand down, Sam, like, released me from duty, and it seems just from what I've heard from Hannah that your father, well, your father..."

"Has never released me," I finish his sentence. "But now...he sort of has, maybe...in the worst way possible."

I put my head in my hands. "Sorry, this is all so much. Can you stop the car? My mind is all kind of jumbled. I think I just need to think on my own for a second."

"For sure," Lachlan says, pulling over as we approach a pedestrian overpass.

I get out of the car and walk halfway across the overpass. I lean over the railing and watch the cars. The lives whizz by, all of them completely unaware of the challenges I'm facing. I feel frozen.

"Charlie?"

I don't know how much time has passed. Lachlan is out of the car now but standing at a distance. "You okay?"

I turn and look at him. "I think I need to call my mother. That might change things."

"No problem," he says, coming closer. "Whatever works."

I take a deep breath. "And I...I also just found out my dad tried to commit suicide when I was twelve."

"Whoa," he says. "That's—I don't know what to say. You didn't know until...?"

I nod. "Today. My grandpa told me."

Lachlan steps beside me and looks out over the highway.

"I'm so furious at both of my parents," I add. "How could they both lie to me like that?"

We stand shoulder to shoulder in silence.

"But I've also been fighting this feeling about my mom," I say finally, "ever since Dad took off, because now I know she's been dealing with a ton, and I realize I miss her so much. But that's like admitting maybe I've been wrong about some things. Really wrong."

My eyes are starting to well up. "Because—not only do I need her, but I think I really really need to not live with my dad. And that seems like the worst conclusion to come to, given where we are right now. What if my dad is...has...taken his life? I just couldn't. I'm terrified, Lachlan."

Lachlan nods and waits for a few moments as I wipe my tears away. The windy rush of the cars wallops the underside of the overpass.

He puts a hand on my arm and says, "What was your dad like when you saw him last?"

I conjure his face. "Happy. Excited." Maybe also manic, but I don't say this.

"I think we should go with that for right now and go find him."

Yes, it feels like Lachlan may be right. Why can't Dad just be free and happy without his illness getting in the way?

"Maybe," I say, brightening a little, "maybe I'm just holding on to caring for my dad. And maybe he doesn't even need me to."

He considers this for a moment and then says, "I think you're right."

"What do you mean?"

"Everything you've said makes sense. But mostly I think that maybe calling your mother is a really good idea."

I turn toward him, and we hug. A long firm hug but somehow gentle. My senses are flooded. With sadness and with joy. A mixture so overwhelming, I push myself away from him.

Then I take out my phone and turn back toward the bustling highway.

Chapter Twelve

The phone rings once and then I hear her voice. "Charlie! Thank God. Where are you now?"

"Mom," I say, trying to be calm, "I really need your help, and I need this to be just about helping Dad. Can you do that?"

There's a long pause.

"Okay," she finally says. "What's going on and where are you?"

"We are at some overpass about ten minutes away from Grandpa's."

"Who is we?"

"Me and Lachlan. A friend. Where are you?"

"I'm ten minutes out. Your grandpa just called me. He said you just disappeared. Like Dad. What's going on?"

"Where *were* you?"

"I...I was also with a friend," she admits and then sighs. "Let's focus on Dad right now, okay? I'll tell you everything when I see you. Why did you leave Grandpa?"

"He wasn't going to come anyway, and I didn't want to see you."

There's another long pause. "Where are you exactly?"

I look around for highway signs. "We're at the junction of highway 10 and 44. Lachlan was going to come to Calm Lake with me because we think Dad is there and that he's not in a good way."

"Grandpa told me that," she says, "but I want *you* to tell me everything that's happened."

"Okay, Dad disappeared yesterday, and he had looked up a canoe outfitter on his laptop, and he hasn't taken his pills for at least forty-eight hours."

"How do you know that?"

"Because I have them," I say. "Or at least I did. They're at Grandpa's."

I hear her take a breath. "What else?"

"Well, Jordan—oh yeah, I met her, by the way—said something about Dad 'shooting the moon,' and it doesn't make sense but I can't help but think it's important—"

"He said 'shooting the moon'?"

"Yes. You know, from Hearts—"

"I'll be there as soon as possible."

"Okay, but—"

She ends the call.

Ten minutes later Mom's car pulls up in front of us. She gets out of her car, wearing a purple skirt and sneakers.

"I'm having a hard time not completely flipping out on you right now," she snaps. "Leaving the city without telling me. Not telling me your father has gone AWOL. Not telling me he hasn't taken his pills. Is there more?"

"Um," I say, turning to Lachlan. "You should probably go." But I don't want him to.

Lachlan steps bravely toward us.

"Um, I'd like to help if I could," he says. "I'm Lachlan, by the way. I'm in Charlie's math class and I...well, I knew she was in trouble, and I just wanted to help." He stands up taller. "I still want to."

I see Mom's fiery eyes extinguish. I'm not sure if it's his sweetness or the fact that some help may be needed or that she can't think straight, but she nods. "Okay, you can follow us to the park. Thank you."

She turns to me. "Let's go," she orders. I shoot a grateful look at Lachlan and get in her car.

Mom turns the key and immediately speeds off, not even waiting for Lachlan.

"Could you slow down?"

"He'll find us. Lachlan is apparently very resourceful."

This makes me angry. "Dad tried to commit suicide four years ago, didn't he?"

Mom's face falls. "That...we had a good reason not to—"

"*Don't* do that, Mom. And don't try to get out of it. You lied to me. The big truth teller lied."

"Ugh!" Mom moans. "We need to focus. I called the RCMP, but I don't think they took me seriously. A woman concerned because her bipolar ex has gone on a canoe trip alone. Anyway, they said it would be quicker to call the park ranger. I tried the park, but there was no answer. Now please take my phone and give me directions."

She's holding the phone out, but I don't want to take it. I don't want to give her even an inch.

But she's right. Whatever I feel right now, we just have to move. Without a word, I snatch the phone from her and start searching.

Chapter Thirteen

When we arrive at the park office, Mom jumps out and starts heading toward the building.

"We should wait for Lachlan," I call out, but she doesn't respond, which infuriates me.

I see Lachlan's car come around the corner, so I decide to wait.

When he gets out, he says, "Your mom?"

"Already inside," I say with a shrug.

"I was thinking," Lachlan says, "I want to help out, I really do, but I'm like, not a knight in shining armor or anything, you know? Here to save the damsel in distress."

I laugh. I actually think he is, but I also know what he means.

"And," he adds, "it seems as if you and your mom, well, kinda need to work out a few things."

I laugh again. I'm amazed by Lachlan, and I'm suddenly overcome with emotion. I step toward him and hug him hard, and then, without thinking, I pull back and kiss him on the lips.

He's surprised and so am I. We look at each other and smile. I move toward him for something less rushed just as my mother shoves the park office door open.

"Your dad's here," she says. "They told me he booked a site on Calm Lake. I arranged gear for us. The canoe and everything is being readied on the dock. It'll take us about four hours to get there."

It looks like she's bought a red nylon top and green shorts.

"I also talked to Grandpa," she says. "He wants to come, but his truck won't start. I don't know what—"

"I was going to suggest," Lachlan interrupts, looking at her and then me, "that I go get the medication Charlie left at the cottage. So while I do that, I could get your grandpa too, if that works."

"That," Mom says, "is a wonderful idea, Lachlan."

I smile.

"Okay," he says with a nod. I'm hoping for another hug, but he puts a hand on my shoulder, turns and goes to his car.

When we get to the dock, I untie the boat filled with gear. Mom moves to the back.

"I'm sterning," I say firmly.

"No, you are not," she says, getting in. "You forget I led trips in Quetico when I was your age."

I give her a deadly stare and get into the bow.

I begin paddling as hard as I can, pushing all my emotions into every stroke. I see a few other canoes passing us at a distance. We are moving fast across the large lake, with the wind racing at our backs. Still it takes us about an hour. As we get closer to land, our strokes slow. I direct the boat through some low rocks in the shallows until it hits the sandy shore of the portage.

"What does 'shooting the moon' mean?" I ask, without moving.

"Not now," she says firmly. "After the portage."

"And what about your friend?"

"Charlie!" she yells and jumps out of the boat. "Enough. It's not time. You didn't speak to me the whole way across the lake, and that's just fine, because what we need to do is get to Daddy as soon as we can."

The word *Daddy* hits me in the throat.

"Honey," she says, seeing my face. "I know. This is hard for me too. I loved your dad. Love him. We had so many good times. Fun times."

She lets me process that for a second.

"It's just over this portage. We need to be fast, Charlie. We're trying to save your father's life right now."

These words crash hard against me—*my father's life.* I know this is what is at stake, but hearing her say it is terrifying.

We lift the canoe and hurry over the flat, rocky path. The forest finally opens up, and the shore on this side is steeper and rockier. As Mom steps into the water, I see short wavy hairs of algae clinging to the rocks. I'm about to warn her when she falls backward.

I drop the canoe and run to her.

I reach down. "Mom! Are you all right?"

"Yes, yes," she mumbles. "I'm fine."

"You don't look fine."

"My ankle," she admits, wincing.

I carefully strip Mom of her bag. I lift the canoe onto my legs and shuffle over, gently guiding the boat into the water. I throw the packs in.

"These are so light—is there even food in here?" I ask. I feel my hunger rising.

"Yes, somewhere in there."

"Okay." I'm worried about her—and our journey. "We'll have that later."

The water in this bay looks mostly calm. Little ripples race across the surface of the water.

"Are you okay to get in the canoe?" I ask.

She pauses.

"We can wait," I add, "but—"

"No, no," she insists, "I just...Charlie, I just need a little help."

I can hear a crack in her voice, and I realize, for maybe the first time, that this stubborn streak not only tears us apart. It also binds us. I take her forearm, and I lift and guide her into the boat.

I read the map, which Grandpa taught me to do. I'm figuring out how the coast matches the map, and how the contour lines show where hills and cliffs should show up.

Mom doesn't pick up her paddle at first, so I begin on my own.

"Mom, are you okay?"

"I think it's a bad sprain. I'm sorry. I'm sorry about everything, Charlie. We shouldn't have lied. It's just that once we did, it became a bit of a trap. Then, once I left your Dad, I felt that telling you would make you think I was blaming him or trying to get you back."

I keep paddling, not knowing what to say. I wasn't expecting this.

So I stare at the map and try to figure out where we go next.

Chapter Fourteen

We paddle and paddle. The strokes make whooshing sounds in the water, and the sun quietly prickles my skin. Sweat rolls down the small of my back.

"Your father," Mom says out of nowhere, setting down her paddle, "he always worried you'd turn out like him."

I sort of knew this before but not exactly. It was my worry too—one of them anyway—and I think it maybe made me want to control things. Him and his sickness. But something has shifted.

"When you were just a baby," she continues, turning in her seat, "he'd peer into your eyes. I knew he was worrying and wondering, who would you be? Was it right for him to have a child, knowing what might be in store for you too?"

"What about you?" I ask. "Did you ever worry about that?"

"No," she replies. "I always felt you'd be like me."

She puts her paddle to the side and leans back on the pack. "My ankle is bad," she says.

Neither of us speak for a few minutes, and then I say, "I think I've always been trying to be like Dad, be as genius as him, even though I'm probably more like you."

"Maybe. I don't know," she says. "You are pretty genius all on your own."

Then her head tips back a little bit. Her eyes are closed, her expression flat.

I continue to paddle. We are at least another forty-five minutes from the next portage.

I glance at Mom and realize she's asleep. What if she's gotten too much sun? Or hit her head when she fell?

"Mom, are you okay?"

"Yes, fine."

"Okay, then. When's your birthday?"

"Charlie," she scolds, then finally sighs. "June 24, 1967. The summer of love...so I must be full of it."

"Then Dad says, 'You're full of it, all right.'"

"And then I say, 'I'm full of beans.'"

"And then he says, 'That's not good! They always give you the farts.'"

"And then you laugh," she says, her tone changing. "Or later you roll your eyes. Or even later say, 'You guys are soooo pathetic.'"

"Yeah."

Even this, even them being so stupidly cute, and me being so stupidly mean, seems like the best time ever.

"Mom?"

"Yes?"

"Who's your new friend?"

She thinks for a moment and then says, "His name is Marco. And he's nice."

"Nice."

"Yeah, nice. I'm learning it's a pretty good quality in a man."

I think of Lachlan. He's nice—and so much more.

"I get it," I say. "Nice like not like Dad."

She considers this.

"Yes," she finally admits, and I realize this doesn't make me as sad as I thought it might.

There's a blister rising on my thumb. I feel light-headed.

"That was a big sigh," my mom says, lifting in her seat. "Are you all right, honey?"

"No," I say, "I'm not. I'm tired. Tired of all this. I can't take care of you and Dad and pretend everything is going to be okay. I can't pretend I don't love you anymore." I start to cry. "I am just so angry at Dad, so totally furious, because why the hell are we even here!"

Without saying anything, Mom sits up, unzips her pack and grabs a bag of trail mix. She tosses it toward me.

"Eat," she says.

I don't argue. I take a big handful.

"Can you fill the water bottle? I'll get the iodine pills."

I can see my mom wants to take care of me. And it feels good.

She reaches for a few energy bars. She tosses one to me and rips hers open. Then she finds her bottle of ibuprofen.

We eat in silence.

"Okay," she says. "Let's paddle."

We start up again at a solid, consistent pace. After a while my mom stops and turns herself fully around.

"Water's ready now." She takes takes a pill out

of the bottle, has a big swig and then passes it over to me. I glug the water down. It tastes gross—and delicious.

"I'm going to tell you some things now. I'm sorry I didn't earlier."

"Okay." I stop paddling and we drift.

"Your father tried to tell me he was going to do this."

"Do what?"

"I'm afraid it's not going to make sense to you."

"Don't talk down to me, Mom. Just tell me."

"Okay," she agrees with a nod. "He told me he wasn't sure if he could do it anymore."

"Do what?"

"Take care of you, but I think it's not what he really meant."

"Mom," I say, "tell me. What is shooting the moon?"

"When your father was young," she replies, "maybe twelve or thirteen, he was just starting to accept that he was different and that life wasn't going to be easy for him. And he began to have thoughts. Bad thoughts."

She swallows deeply.

"Once when he and your grandpa were on a trip together, he had a sudden thought, or idea, in the water."

"Grandpa told me—after Dad smashed through the library door."

"Yes, while he was in the water, your father thought about ending his life. Going to the other side. Shooting the moon. For him it always meant going for broke, trying to solve a math puzzle, even if it meant he wasn't going to come out the other side."

I can't breathe.

"And the crazy thing is," she says softly, "he said it was the most beautiful idea to him, like it arrived almost like a jewel in his hand. It was his way out."

I pick up my paddle but don't make a stroke.

"He almost did it that day," she says, "but something stopped him. He didn't know what it was."

She is weeping now, and this makes me paddle.

"And when you were born," she says, wiping her eyes, "he found the reason. You were the reason for him to live." She forces a smile. "It mostly worked."

I stay silent.

"When he couldn't even apply for the teaching job, I think he just gave up. His letting go of you, Charlie, and his coming here—I don't understand it completely. I just...I don't know what we are going to find, and I'm scared."

"He didn't let go of me, Mom," I insist. "Don't say that. Shooting the moon is trying to win, not lose," and then I stab the water with my paddle. Over and over.

My mom goes to say something but stops.

She turns and also starts to paddle.

There's nothing more to say.

Chapter Fifteen

The sun is high, so it must be around noon. Every once in a while, I glance at the map, unable to avoid looking at the massive portage ahead of me. It is more than a mile and half long. I don't think Mom can walk that far. I don't know if I can.

I find myself thinking of Lachlan, his button nose and his smile. When I see him in my mind's eye, there's no context. It's just him. Like my brain is unable to place him in anything but the unknown future.

My muscles ache. Each stroke is pain. My blister is now bloody. My shoulder and butt are sore. Without saying a word, Mom drops her paddle and passes me the water.

I'm not mad at her anymore. We are a team. The team we've always been.

As the portage comes into focus, my energy rises. We finally arrive at a sandy beach. Mom hobbles carefully on her ankle.

"You can't come with me," I say.

"I'll try," she argues.

"He's on the next lake, a mile and half away. I'm taking the canoe and a paddle. You are staying."

She pauses, then says, "You need some water and dried food. We can attach it to the seats."

"Good." I drag the canoe up, and Mom stuffs the plastic bag.

We decide I must have the canoe on my shoulders first. I pick it up and swing it on my shoulders. Mom awkwardly dips underneath and attaches everything, including the paddle, which she straps to the seat and the thwart, the narrow beam that supports the middle of the boat. When she's done, she gets out from under the canoe and sits down. All I can see are her soggy sneakers and her swollen ankle.

"Okay, Charlie," says her voice. "I know you can do this."

"Thanks, Mom," I say. I have the urge to hug her.

"I love you," she says.

"I love you too, and I'm sorry," I say. "I'm so—"

"It's okay, Charlie. It's okay. You need to go. I'll make a fire. There'll be food when you get back."

I start to walk. At first the path is steep, and I don't know how I'm possibly going to portage all the way. When I get to the top of a crest, I see that the path flattens out. It is well worn and wide. Once I catch my breath, I feel newly energized. Before long, though, my shoulders and neck are killing me.

There's a clearing up ahead, and I figure I'm a third of the way.

Ping.

It's my phone. I had forgotten I had it. I guess the higher elevation and clearing has allowed a message to come through. I can't get it while carrying the canoe.

I shuffle more quickly. Grandpa always said you should go as fast as you can when you portage but with as little bumping up and down as possible. I pick up speed and confidence and then suddenly—*BOOM!*

I stop on the spot, pain shooting through my shoulder, the canoe shuddering over top of me. It falls to the side, almost carrying me down with it. I dip away as the canoe crashes and bounces on the ground, hitting a rock.

In shock, I look up. There is a small turn in the portage path, and a great big white cedar in the middle of it. I see that I hit it straight on.

I glance back at the canoe. I know I won't pick it up again. I'm just too tired. How am I going to get to Dad? I start to cry, and then I'm sobbing. I don't even feel like moving.

I hear another *ping*.

I dig my hand into my pocket and lift the phone.

It's Lachlan. **I hope you're doing okay, XOXOX**.

My face flushes. I am embarrassed, even in the middle of nowhere, but thrilled—and it gives me a burst of hope.

I pull the map out of my back pocket. The portage appears to veer to the right a ways from here. If I cut through the woods, it would shorten my trip—it would be like walking the hypotenuse of a right triangle.

I can see my dad's eyes light up at the idea.

Yes! he would say. *We can do it and we will save time!*

I can also see my grandpa frowning, saying, *The Indigenous Peoples of this area have been portaging the land forever. If there were a better way, it would have been found thousands of years ago.*

I can also hear myself arguing with my father. "We don't have a compass, so we won't even know if we get off track."

Suddenly I scream, "STOP!"

To get them out of my head.

I'm bent over now.

There's nothing—only birds in the forest. And me.

Finally I stand up. I grab the food and water and start along the well-worn path. At first I walk and then I begin to jog, knowing I've made the right choice. Mine.

Chapter Sixteen

Ahead through the trees, I see the lake. I race down the rocky trail. I almost fall several times. My heart is pounding with fear and joy. I finally arrive at the end of the portage, a small, marshy lake.

The first thing I see is a blue canoe across the water, maybe 150 yards away. The canoe is pulled up on the side of a campsite. I see the flash of Dad's red tent. And blue-gray smoke coming up through the trees.

Next thing I know, I'm taking my clothes off, down to my bra and underwear, and slipping into the reeds and muck.

As I become submerged, the water hugs me tightly—the water that once tried to claim my father's life.

I am doing the front crawl. My heart races. I can't hear anything but the splashing of water. I look up. The lake is small, but swimming it feels far enough.

I finally arrive at the shallows of the shore, rising up like a swamp monster.

I am too afraid to call out.

The fire is behind a pine tree. I see a paddle against it and a green pack I don't recognize. Suddenly I think that maybe this isn't Dad. We've gotten it all wrong. I'm in my underwear and bra in the middle of nowhere.

I go up the rocky shore in my bare feet, covering my chest. I come around the tree and see a man sitting on a log bench, his back to me, next to the fire.

He's in a red windbreaker, new-looking. He's hunched.

It can't be Dad.

Is it?

"Dad?" I call out softly.

The man turns, and even after he does, I don't know it's him for a few seconds. The face is distorted. It's not his wet hair, it's not his patchy salt-and-pepper beard. It's the eyes. My dad's eyes. They are dead.

"Dad?" I say, begging a bit.

He turns slowly. "Sweetie," he mumbles, looking through me, vague and dreamy. He doesn't get up.

I run to him and I squeeze him hard, but his body feels lifeless. I pull back and try to look him in the eyes.

"Why?" I ask, giving him a shake, desperate and confused.

He stares at me emptily. So I go grab a towel off the line and find a fleece in his tent. I put it on. I sit beside my dad. Together we stare at the dying fire, because I'm not sure what else we can do. I hear the flap of a bird exiting the water. And the wind way up in the trees.

Finally he clears his throat and then speaks, thick and slow. "I was wrong."

"What about, Dad?"

He doesn't take his eyes off the fire.

"Last time I was here, I was twelve. I thought of taking my life. And this time I thought...I thought if I returned, I could undo it somehow. Start over again. Start from the beginning. I was sure of it. But it's impossible. It's just—"

"Dad."

"I knew you would come," he continues. "It makes me so happy...and so sad too."

A pause. Then a breath.

These words wake me, make my shoulders rise.

A log crackles in the firepit.

I wait for Dad to say something more. But he doesn't.

"I met Jordan," I say. "And she told me about you not even applying for the job at the university. That kinda sucked to find out. The lies and this wild goose chase. Everything. But none of that really matters. You are alive. And I know—well, I learned today that you haven't always made that choice."

His stillness constricts.

"But what I've learned over the last twenty-four hours is that I...I know...I know I need to start making my own choices, and one of those is that I think I need to live with Mom."

My heart is in my throat.

We stare into the smoldering ashes of the fire.

Until his body finally releases.

I risk a glance at him.

I see his eyes, and in them, I see the smallest smile. And it means that all he wants is the best for me.

And just then we hear it. A word. An echoing voice.

"Hello!" it says.

Dad looks over his shoulder, and I jump up and run to the shore.

Across the lake, her new red shirt in a background of gray and green.

"It's Mom." I call back to her with delight. "MOM!"

I call out again. "MOM!!"

She waves.

I turn back to Dad, who is also up on his feet, shuffling like an old man. He smiles at me, and I say with wonder, "She's amazing."

He nods. "Yes."

I hurry back to the tree. "I'm going to go get her," I say, grabbing the paddle.

Running down to the shore, I flip Dad's canoe onto my thighs. I slide it into the water, follow it and then hop in like a pro.

As the canoe glides, I turn back to Dad, who is sitting on a rock, grinning. With pride?

I get on my knees and perform a nice, deep J-stroke, making an S, left then right, through the water.

I do it again.

And again, the S getting slimmer. The line getting straighter. The speed picking up. I am soloing for the first time in years. I can feel the water on my fingers and the sharp pain in my shoulders and my heart fully alive.

I am leaving my father and heading toward my mother, but for now, I promise myself, closing my eyes, I'm steering my very own path from here to there.

It feels good.

After a while I open my eyes and see that I'm off course.

And I smile.

Epilogue

We are back in Toronto, and everything is different but fine.

Everybody's safe.

I am at Mom's place now, studying math alone in her kitchen.

Dad is back on his meds and back at his apartment after a twenty-four-hour stay at the hospital.

We've talked twice on the phone since we all returned from Calm Lake. It's really hard to stop myself from running out the door and just being with him, but I have to trust that he can take care of himself.

He's applied to teach part time at a college in the suburbs that Jordan told him about. Dad admitted to me that he was always running away from the hard stuff like teaching and parenting. That's what his real job is now, he says, to do the difficult things. I'm hopeful, but I'm not exactly holding my breath. I'm with Mom for now.

The three of us managed to get back across the long portage without our canoes, and there was a ranger waiting for us with a power boat. Grandpa was at the dock, his arms crossed. He gave Dad a big hug, though, and I think I saw tears in both of their eyes. Grandpa said that Lachlan had needed to get back home and what a fine young man he was. Mom and I drove home together, and with two hours on the road, we were able to work out some things. I told her I wasn't theoretically against this new nice guy, Marco, and I told her more about Lachlan, whom I texted to say that all was okay.

Speaking of Lachlan, we finally had our smoothie. I am embarrassingly in love, but we are both buckling down for exams.

I now look at my phone beside me, which I try to have off while I'm studying math. I see there's a message from Hannah. **How goes the battle?**

And one from Lachlan. **One day to go, C!**

That's what he calls me now, C. It makes me smile every time.

I answer Hannah first. **Terrible. still stuck on math. Functions.**

Sorry, no help here!

I glance at Lachlan's message. I should ask him to help me, but I just can't. I want to do this on my own. I reply to his message. **I know. Can't wait to see you when this is all over.**

I continue to stare at my phone, waiting for a response.

Nothing. He's probably studying too.

I look at my math. A question I can't quite get my mind around no matter how many times I try to practice it.

I look back at my phone. There's a message.

Testing testing.

I don't know the number. **Is there anybody out there?**

What idiot doesn't say who they are when they are contacting someone new on a cell?

> **Is this the number of the smartest most incredible young woman on Earth?** it says.

Dad?!?!?!?!?!?!?

> **Yep, that's me!**

You have a cell phone? are you freaking kidding me?! a cell phone?!?!?

> **Yep, I'm joining the new millennium. I need some way to stay in touch with you, kid. How do I look?**

Not bad, not bad at all...welcome to the wireless world, Dad!

I'm completely blown away—not just by him actually getting a cell phone but also by how it makes me feel. Loved. Dad got a cell phone to connect with me.

So...whaddya wanna talk about? I type with a grin on my face.

> **Well, I have a plan...and I was wondering if you could help me?**

I deflate just a little. A plan. A plan always means trouble with Dad.

Maybe Dad senses this in my lack of response.

> **My new project is proving difficult.**

What project? Can he feel my disappointment between the lines?

> **Teaching math. I got the job and need someone to practice on. Not sure if I'm going to get it right. And I'm scared.**

My heart goes tight.

You are going to teach me math? Even as I type this, I fear I'm wrong.

If you'll have me...Actually, you'll probably need to come over here.

Over to his apartment? Where I used to live?

This feels dangerous, like going backward. **okay, but I'll have to check with mom.**

There's a pause. Is he angry? Hurt? **It's already been done, Charlie. She thinks it's a great idea.**

Now I'm bursting. There are real happy tears now as I type: **I would ❤ that. Do you know anything about functions?**

I just might 😉

You just texted me an emoji! I'm pinching myself. Is this real?

It's real, Charlie...and it won't always be easy.

I can handle that.

I wait a few moments for his next message, which finally comes.

♥ u & ∞ always. C u soon. (This texting is actually kind of fun.)

Matt Beam is a writer, educator and photographer. He has written four YA and middle-grade novels, and published two photographic picture books. Matt has lived in several countries, including Guatemala, New Zealand and Australia, and in Vancouver, British Columbia. He now teaches at an elementary school dedicated to teaching students with dyslexia. He lives in Toronto with his family.

If you or someone you love needs helps with any of the issues discussed in this book, please contact:

In Canada

KidsHelpPhone

kidshelpphone.ca

Call: 1 800-668-6868

Text:686868

In the USA

Teenline

teenline.org

Call: 1-800-852-8336

Text: 839863

Or talk to a trusted adult such as a parent, doctor, teacher, or friend.